PIGS TO THE RESCUE

John Himmelman

Henry Holt and Company

New York

Henry Holt and Company, LLC, *Publishers since 1866* , 175 Fifth Avenue, New York, New York 10010 [www.HenryHoltKids.com]

Henry Holt® is a registered trademark of Henry Holt and Company, LLC.
Copyright © 2010 John Himmelman. All rights reserved. Distributed in Canada by H. B. Fenn and Company Ltd.

Library of Congress Cataloging-in-Publication Data
Himmelman, John.
Pigs to the rescue / John Himmelman. — 1st ed.   p.   cm.
Summary: All week long the pigs help out around the farm in unexpected ways.
ISBN 978-0-8050-8683-6
[1. Pigs—Fiction. 2. Farm life—Fiction.] I. Title.   PZ7.H5686Ph 2010   [E]—dc22   2009006209

First Edition—2010 / Black Prisma color pencil for the outline and watercolor paint were used to create the illustrations for this book.
Printed in May 2010 in the United States of America by Worzalla, Stevens Point, Wisconsin, on acid-free paper. ∞

3 5 7 9 10 8 6 4 2

For Carole,
who wants to help animals

On Monday, the tractor broke down.
Farmer Greenstalk couldn't plow his fields.

"Um, thank you, I think," said Farmer Greenstalk.

On Tuesday, Mrs. Greenstalk found a leak in her garden hose.

Pigs to the rescue!

"You *really* didn't have to do that,"
said Mrs. Greenstalk. "But thanks."

On Wednesday, Jeffrey Greenstalk got his kite stuck in a tree.

Pigs to the rescue!

"Well, you did get it out of the tree,
I guess," said Jeffrey.

On Thursday morning, Caleb the rooster had a sore throat and couldn't crow.

Pigs to the rescue!

"We're awake! We're awake!"
shouted Farmer Greenstalk.

On Friday, Emily Greenstalk broke the lace on her shoe.

Pigs to the rescue!

"Mmph," said Emily.

On Saturday, Ernie the duck was sad
because no one remembered his birthday.

Pigs to the rescue!

"Quack," said Ernie the duck.

On Sunday, Lulu the cat tipped over her saucer of milk.

The Greenstalks ran into the room. "SSHHHHHH," they said.
"Don't let the pigs know!" Everyone froze and listened.

"That was close," said Mrs. Greenstalk.
"Thank goodness, the pigs didn't find out about this one."